Love,
Life's Endless Destiny

Love,
Life's Endless Destiny

Belle Chisholm

Love, Life's Endless Destiny

Copyright © 2021 by Vera Akomah. All rights reserved.

No part of this publication may be reproduced, stored in a retrieval system or transmitted in any way by any means, electronic, mechanical, photocopy, recording or otherwise without the prior permission of the author except as provided by USA copyright law.

The opinions expressed by the author are not necessarily those of URLink Print and Media.

1603 Capitol Ave., Suite 310 Cheyenne, Wyoming USA 82001
1-888-980-6523 | admin@urlinkpublishing.com

URLink Print and Media is committed to excellence in the publishing industry.

Book design copyright © 2021 by URLink Print and Media. All rights reserved.

Published in the United States of America

Library of Congress Control Number: 2021913415
ISBN 978-1-64753-872-9 (Paperback)
ISBN 978-1-64753-873-6 (Digital)

15.06.21

CHAPTER

One

As I look out on the slow tide receding from the coast line along the beach. Asia and Diego both enjoying themselves splashing in the water. To think when we first got here they both were very apprehensive about going near the water.

Finally, Diego as always followed me in as I decided to walk closer to the water in my bare feet. Asia as always moving slowly showing her age is catching up with her as she tends to want to follow me to the water to lie in the coolness of the morning sun.

As I walked along the beach on my daily walk my thoughts drift back to what a wonderful life I've had. Here I was at our summer place in Norfolk, VA just enjoying life as retired couples should. My thoughts went back to when I was a little girl growing up on that hill in Charlottesville. We headed back towards the summer house as the sun began to move to its position just above the water.

The summer house was a large seven bedroom house with a huge kitchen and an extended deck that wrapped around the external that looked out on the ocean. Daniel had it built as a promise he made several years ago. This would be our get away from the company. It never turned out that way, whenever we travel it was always the crew and some crisis that needed his attention.

As I lay on the deck in my favorite chaise, resting my eyes from the walk, Daniel walked out on the deck and asked, "What you thinking about?" "Our life together it has been an interesting journey and the route my life has taken" He smiled and said "Our journey together has been our destiny from the very beginning, but, don't let me interrupt you, I'm going for a walk" as he kissed the top of my head and walked down the steps onto the beach.

I laid my head back on the seat and drifted off in my thoughts. The fourth of July would bring the family together for the holiday. We look forward to seeing the family and the grandchildren. Trinity and Krystyna came up to spend the summer with their Nana.

They both have grown into two beautiful young ladies. They loved visiting us at the summer home. Trinity now going into Army as a veterinarian and Krystyna in her first year of college majoring in journalism. They fulfilled my life during those empty years before that trip to DC.

Then unexpectedly Daniel and I came across each other in the most unusual way. That moment changed both our lives forever. Now here I was planning our tenth wedding anniversary with all the family and extended family in attendance.

Daniel came back after his short walk. I told him Soup had called and said he had prepared the menu for the holiday guest and wanted us to look it over. As I mentioned it to Daniel, and as always he would say, replying somewhat irritated, "Isn't that's why we pay Soup to make these kinds of decisions." "He just wants our approval as always." "Just make it an old fashion military shindig like we used to do on active duty."

I asked him did he miss being a Command Sergeant Major in the Army. He said, "Not really I've never really left the Army considering what I do in my civilian life. DJ now a Sergeant Major and soon will be a CSM himself at his young age of twenty-eight. He kind of reminds me of his dad. I never left the Army it still runs in the family. Trinity pregnant with twins, I just don't know, it's something about twins running in this family. They all come in twos." We both laugh. He said, "It must be in the genes." "Well, all I can say is you always wanted a big family now you got one, grandpa or should I say great grandpa.

So when are Eloise and Chief coming up?" "They're flying up tomorrow we have somethings to go over. Tom is coming with them since Diane living with her family in Seattle. Jai should be here later this evening." "So, what you having, a big "Pow Wow" for Mr. Chairman?" "You may want to be in on this." "So what the big meeting all about?" "We're about to make some leadership changes in the company."

"What type of leadership?" "I thought you wanted to keep the company in the family. Seems to me everyone has their lives already in place. So where or why is it we need new leadership?" "Tom wants to leave the company because Diane's filing for divorce and wants a severance package from the company if she divorces him for mental cruelty."

"Divorce, on the grounds of what, mental cruelty. In what way did the company cause her mental cruelty?" "We believe it has something to do with the house Janelle left to her when I had it demoed." "So, is this the so called mental cruelty she's basing this on."

"This is something she felt was due to her and I had the company demolished it so she couldn't have it. She found out I had the company demo it because when I brought the house for Janelle it was brought under my name not the company's name. When I started the company I transferred ownership under the company's name after our divorce. So when I demo it, I demoed it under the company's name.

So what she found out by some lawyer her father found for her she was entitled to a severance package from the company after I did what I had to do. What I should have done was give her that burnt out piece of ruins." "But, Daniel Janelle didn't own the house, you did."

"That's beside the point honey, she's willing to settle for a settlement of two hundred thousand dollars for the ruins and another hundred thousand for the mental anguish. Creating the emotional and psychological distress she went through caused by the company her husband worked for. So she's asking for three hundred thousand dollar settlement from the company.

If we don't give her that severance package or settlement she's going to take us to court and say we were the cause of her mental instability.

We are the cause of her divorce and the medical treatment because of her unstable mental condition." "Daniel, I don't understand, why not just give her the settlement so we can get her off our back and Tom can get on with his life. Plus that small amount of money is just pennies compare to what the company's worth is."

"Honey, I understand but it's the principle of the matter. Diane has no idea what the company's worth. She's doing this because of her father and plus it's her way of getting back at us. She never wanted to come here. She came here hoping she was able to get you back for what you did to Janelle.

Also along with Tom's ultimatum, he was going to leave her if she didn't come with him to Texas. She made that choice she didn't have to come to Texas." "I still don't understand we didn't do anything to either of them.

They did it to themselves. Diane with her conniving deceitful ways and Janelle blaming everyone for her not taking care of herself. Now she thinks we owe her something. I feel really sorry for her. Jealousy has almost destroyed her too."

"Diane thinks you married me for my money. Janelle had convinced her of that when she heard we got married." "I never knew you were wealthy when we met at Arlington. You found me. I didn't find you."

"Honey, you know this all goes back to when you were at the Presidio. Tom would always speak highly of you and she did not like it." "So what is this meeting about?" "We need to decide how we're going to handle this Diane situation. We need to decide if we want to do a settlement or go to court. I for one want to go to court, but it falls on the court to see if she can prove what she claims is true.

For one thing Diane came here with a mental condition, bipolar and an alcoholic problem. The thing about this is do we want to subject Tom to all this reticule, bad publicity and court case. This could all fall back on us and the corporation in the long run. This is the main reason for this meeting. Tom has been a close friend and loyal member of this company and we do not want to subject him to this type of scrutiny.

Whatever we decide on it has to be voted on by all the shareholders or should I say board members. That is why we're having this so call board meeting. DJ can't be here so I will be his proxy." "So, are we voting to give her what she wants or demanding?" "No, we're not.

We're voting to give her what we are willing to offer her in a severance package and it will in no way be anything close to three hundred thousand dollars. She never did anything for this company as a spouse but caused havoc for it. Her divorce settlement with Tom is between them. We have nothing to do with the problems they had in their marriage.

It is up to me to decide on that amount and only I know why I demolished that house and what it was worth." "So, how much you want to give Diane?" "Whatever we decide on and it's not for the house but for us to get that vicious woman out our lives."

"I never could understand why Diane would want that house so much. She never worked a day in her life. All she's ever been was a military's spouse. Diane and Janelle were just alike looking for someone to take care of them. That is so typical for her kind." "Val, honey they were like leaches draining the life out of those around them."

"So Daniel, why did you demoed that house, it could have been repaired." "I had too many bad memories and after I found out later what she did to my two children, I'm damn glad I did. I did not want any memories of life in that house with her. Val, knowing what she did to those kids, do you actually think I could live with that house still standing.

All that went on in that house even with what I later found out. No way, I'm glad it's gone and Diane best be glad I didn't put a stick of explosive in there myself." "I see you still haven't got over what she did." "No, I haven't and probably never will. I'm having a hard time trying to forgive her. I can't think of anything that could make a person do what she did to our son and daughter.

That's why they never wanted to go home." "Daniel, you have to find a way to forgive her. You have to start by forgiving yourself. Knowing and being married to you I know you blame yourself for what they went through." "I can't help how selfish I was for not having brought my kids with me.

All I wanted was to just get away from Janelle. She was very toxic when it came to being around her. I tried for the kids but she made me not want to come home. The worse part about that is I had a feeling she mistreated them. I just wanted to believe she loved them. It made me feel better about what I was doing with my misconceptions of me being a good husband, provider and father.

It was my fault my children went through that. I can't blame anyone but myself and I can never forgive myself for not being there when I should had been. Out of all my accomplishment and as wealthy as I am, I cannot forgive myself for what I did to my children.

Val, that pain cuts so deep in my heart, there is nothing no one can say or do for me to ever forgive myself. Val, I tried but it always comes out as selfish reasons and excuses for what I allow happened. Val, I can't forgive myself, so how can I forgive Janelle."

"Daniel, Janelle was a narcissistic individual with bipolar tendencies who cared only about herself and I imagine she didn't really love DJ. She used her son DJ to satisfy her own selfish perverted behavior.

Daniel this is no longer about Janelle. It's about you and how long you are going to continue to hold this unforgiveness in your heart for yourself. That hold is not Janelle, it's you who won't allow you to forgive yourself and you are blaming her. Daniel, she's dead and gone.

You have people who are here for you. Who love you and won't allow that to happen." "I know Val, maybe one day I will. See it's been six years since her death and she still got her hold on my life. I just don't know how to let it go to forgive."

"Daniel, go talk to Chaplain Anderson, he's been your friend and spiritual advisor for most of your adult life. Also he knew you and Janelle most of your life. He could have some insight on how you can get through your crisis in trying to forgive her."

"That's just it Val, I don't want to forgive her." "Then you don't want to forgive yourself." "Well, I guess I don't. That's the only way I can face the fact I abandon my children when I knew the type of person Janelle was. I keep asking myself that question over and over again. Why, was I so selfish and self-absorbed in myself? I can't reason it out in no way shape or form. I've tried to think about it.

The worse part about it Val, this all happen way before I met you. I keep asking myself. Where in the hell was my head during that time frame. All those years my children were suffering. I can't get any answers. You know why Val, because there aren't any answers.

There're no excuses for what I had allowed happened." He took a deep breath and said, "Maybe I will, go talk with Chaplain Anderson. I need to find some peace and maybe some forgiveness also. I'll give him a call after this thing with Diane is over with."

"Honey, why don't you call him now? If you wait too long you may decide to put it off again. See if you can get Chief to swing by and pick him up. It'll be nice to see him again.

Now, if you don't. I may take matters in my own hands. You know how I am when I set my mind to something. Just invite him up for the Fourth that way things won't look so conspicuous. You two been friends a long time."

Daniel called Chaplain Anderson and invited him up for the Fourth. His first question was what's wrong Dan? I'll see you in a few days. He knew something was wrong. Daniel never calls him unless it's something bothering him.

CHAPTER

Two

Later that afternoon everyone arrived for the big "Pow Wow". It did not take long for the shareholders to decide on what to do about Diane. We unanimously agreed on giving her a severance package of one hundred and fifty thousand dollars with a "Gag Order" preventing her from discussing or revealing any classified or unclassified information ever disclosed pertaining to HIE, LLC's contracts with the federal government and the department of defense in the past, present or future affiliation with the corporation.

She is restricted from discussing any information pertaining to her future ex-husband association with the corporation during his past and current tenue with the corporation.

Daniel agreed to assist Tom in any monetary support in settling his divorce settlement with his soon to be ex-wife. Daniels incurred this is because he has been a close friend and loyal employee to him and the corporation for a very long time. He and Tom discussed it more off line. Tom agreed to what the shareholders had voted on as a shareholder and he agreed to stay on with the company.

Diane later agreed to what the corporation had offered her. After her lawyers' finding out Daniel had brought the house under a quick sale for way less than it was so called appraised for. He then later had it transferred to the corporation as a tax write off.

Now here we were Charmaine and I planning for the upcoming Fourth of July celebration and the twins now three years old. I finally talked Charmaine into opening her Event planning business. She wasn't that excited about it with the twins until she found a nanny for them. We named it H&H (Harris & Howard) Event Planners. She ran everything from her house and Eloise and I was mostly there as her assistants. The great thing about it was she did the event planning and Soup's Kitchen did the catering service. The whole thing worked out as if it was all planned.

This year's Fourth of July was going to be very spectacular with the boats on the ocean and the fireworks from the town and from the nearby Naval Base. The great thing about being near the military is they always have great fireworks for the Fourth.

All the family would be here and the two day event would end with the fireworks. This would be our second year we celebrated the Fourth at the summer house. Daniel had decided to rent one of the summer cottages for the holiday. The cottage was just two houses down from ours which made it convenient for the overflow of family.

Eloise and Chief had arrived earlier with little Jim. They named him after Jim, James Edward Harris. Chief said we had to give him a name in order to get him a birth certificate. They had to guestimate his birthdate. They think it was round about July when he was born. They made it July 4th. So we decided to celebrate his birthday on the fourth.

Chief said, it fits him, he's such a little firecracker with a lot of energy. Just like his grandpa. We could never make that boy slow down. CSM and I would have to say slowdown Jim-bob before you blow a gasket. It was hard to imagine Jim as a grandfather. I still saw him as a son.

Little Jim had grown so fast. He called Eloise, Auntie Eloise and Chief, Uncle Bernie. He was really attached to them both; but mostly to Chief. Chief called him Sport. Little Jim now almost four would follow Chief everywhere he could. He was closed to his cousins Kevin and Kristina, which Eloise allowed them to have a lot of playdates.

Jim spent a lot of time with the three. He said he wanted them to be raised together even though he was a grandfather now. It reminded him how DJ, Cory and Courtney were when they were at the mansion. I kind of agreed.

Jim having gotten somewhat over his ordeal seems to be handling things much better. He's still very close to Chief and Daniel. I don't think after this nothing could break the bond between those three. For a while there I was very concerned about Jim's and Daniel's relationship.

I mentioned it to Daniel on one of our date nights. He said he wanted to give him a little time to get his family situated. I told him, "Daniel, we're his family also. Jim is just like your son. He was there before I came along. He is a big part of you. I don't understand what's holding you back. This is not like you. What is it with you?" "It's not so much as me. I just don't know how to approach him and not feel I'm prying in his personal business. Every time I ask him how things going he says pretty good.

Last time I asked he said CSM I know how to handle my business. I left it at that." "You left it at what? What is that? What does "that" mean Daniel?" "I don't know Val. It just seems he has some animosity towards me about something.

I have no idea what it could be. I don't know how to ask him without us both flying off at the handle. I don't know how deep or how far back this goes. Val, it hurts me that we've got this gaping hole between us and I don't know how to close it up." I thought to myself, *"I'll get to the bottom of this."*

So I decided to go over to the COC one evening when Chief and Daniel were off on one of their so call excursions. Eloise and Tom were gone for the day. I asked Jim was everything alright. He said everything was just fine. I came straight out and said. "Jim, everything is not just fine.

What's up with you and CSM? He's like a kid that's lost his best friend. And you, you just as bad. You hang over here trying to find something to keep you busy until it's nothing else to do but, go home. What happen to you two? Everyone notice it, if I do. Chief said he hadn't notice anything."

"If you must ask Miss Val, CSM thinks I still have PTSD." Well, do you?" "No, I don't Miss Val." "Why you think he thinks that?" "Because he's always asking me is everything alright." "Maybe he just cares enough for you, to ask you are everything alright. Don't you think he has a right to ask you that?" "No, he doesn't Miss Val. He has no right to ask me that every time he sees me. I can handle my own business."

"Ok, Jim I'm just asking you but, just listen to how you sound. You just went off the handle on me." "Miss Val, no one else ask me how I'm doing or if everything alright." "That's because no one knows you better than Daniel or Chief. Believe me Chief notice, but he's not going to say anything until it gets out of hand."

He then started to cry. This was about the second time since I've known Jim I've seen him cry. I asked him, "You still going to VA for your therapy" He said, "No, I stop when I start going to the Chaplain.

Things started getting really busy with the babies, little Jim, and Stephanie. Then there's Anna calling to check on Stephanie because she won't talk to her mother. No, everything is not alright and I don't know what to do to fix it." "Well, maybe it's not something you can fix by yourself, Jim. That's why you have family. We are here to help you. We are your family.

You have been a part of this family way before any of us came along. Daniel loves you like he loves DJ. Daniel wants to help if you let him. He keeps asking you are everything alright because he knows and feels something is wrong. He wants to help. I know he think he's Mr. Fixit but, that's what he does. He likes being Mr. Fixit especially for people he loves and his family.

Jim you are family. He will do anything in the world for you and I know you know this. I think it's because you want to prove you can handle this. Jim you have too much on your plate to try to fix any of it. Stop trying to prove to yourself that you are just as much man as Chief and CSM. Although you are but, you don't have to prove it to them. They already know this.

The problem is you are trying to prove it to yourself. Then what you do. Come over here to your little hole, the COC and try to cover your hurt by trying to work it out here. Jim, call CSM and Chief and tell them you need to talk to them. Tell them you need their help and see if they don't come running. I want you to call them right now before I leave. I'm going out and call Jai to come pick me up. Jim, call them now, before I leave.

He picked up the phone and called CSM. I heard him through his tears telling CSM. "Man I need your help can you come to the COC." He made the same call to Chief." Just as I walked out the door Jai was pulling up behind Daniel. He asked, "What you doing over here?" I said "I was looking for you." "Now you know you don't go looking for me. What you been up too." I said "Jai's here I'll talk with you later."

Jai asked as we drove off, "Val, what you up to?" "You sound like Daniel" "You still didn't answer my question." "I'm trying to keep my family from falling apart." "Ah, what done happened now?" "I can't tell you but I'm working on it." "I know you are Miss busy body."

"Well, if I don't put my two cents in it I might lose someone that's dear to my heart and I'm determined I won't let that happen." "Who's that Jim?" "I'm not going to say, but you are warm." "I notice he has changed a lot. He's too quiet the way Soup puts it.

Jim never been but so quiet since I've known him coming from Soup." "I know I'm just worried about him. He's got a lot on his plate with all that has happened in his life recently. He needs help and don't want anyone to know it. That's all I'm going to say. I've prayed about it and left it for Daniel and Chief to fix it."

"That's why CSM came over there. He liked to ran over me coming out of the drive way. I thought something had happen." "I think Jim was heading for a meltdown. I had him to call Daniel and Chief before I left the COC. Don't tell anyone what I just told you, Especially Soup!" "I won't." as she dropped me off in front of the mansion.

Daniel came in a couple of hours later. I was in the shower getting ready for bed. I didn't know how long he was going to be out. He came and got in the shower with me and said. "Mother hen, you have been kind of busy." "Now what's that supposed to mean?" "Out there checking on your little chicks?" I got out the shower and said, "Well, someone has to. I've just been concerned about Jim since all this drama has taken place.

We seem to have forgotten about him through all the drama with Stephanie and little Jim as well as the birth of the twins. After our conversation at dinner the other night it struck me. We had thrown Jim issue aside and took up with the other related issues.

We allowed those issues take precedence over what had happened to him and fail to realize they were all related. Jim didn't say anything. He was just trying to figure out what he is supposed to do to fix this whole matter. But what has happened, it has overwhelm him to the point he has no idea what needs to be done.

This is not unusual for a person in his state of mind. The whole thing became out of control when no one was trying to help him to get control of what he was supposed to do next. He was setting back watching all of us do what we thought was helping him instead of assisting him.

When everything quiet down his frame of mind was, what I do next. He had no idea or guidance as given him in past situation with the company. Daniel, he had no guidance how to handle Stephanie's situation.

The situation with little Jim and his own situation for that matter. So, what he did when everything quiet down. He hid his self in the COC away from all that was going on around him.

He knew that there were issues that needed attending to. But, if things were back the way it was before all hell had broken lose, all he had to say was everything was just fine. When in reality, he knew it wasn't. Jim felt if no one said anything. Then everything must be alright. If someone like you asked, then they felt he wasn't handling his business. He had let things go too far, by not asking for assistance.

Daniel, I never seen Jim cried but twice since I've known him. The first was when Stephanie was located and tonight at the COC. I told him to call you and Chief, the two most reliable people he could depend on. Jim was broken, mentally and physically. He needs moral support and he needs to know, that you two guys love and care for him the way you used to.

He wants you to trust him and believe in him as you did before all this happen. I don't know any other way to put this honey. I don't want to wake up and find out some devastating thing has happened because none of us noticed that a love one has PTSD or whatever you want to call it.

That no one cared enough for him to help him get the help he needs." I started to cry, "Daniel, Jim has an overwhelming case of PTSD. He needs both you and Chief to help him get his self together. You two are the only ones he trusts and you two has to be that moral support in his crisis.

Just as I have flashback of Q-Tips demised and you of your son DJ. Jim must have that same flashback and he has not yet talked about it. Remember when I told you, to talk it out. Jim has never done that. Try to find a way to get him to talk about it. He has to talk it out.

One thing the mind won't do is let you forget traumatic incidents. It will continue to spit it out at you. When it does it just get that much painful. That's why you must talk it out or else it will destroy you.

With combat vet when they don't talk about it they began to relive and act it out. You as his friend and closest person to him your job are to listen and not ask question. He must talk it out as it appears in his mind. That's where the trap door is that holds all that painful memory is held. Those memories that must and can only be released by talking about it.

Remember Daniel, I allowed you to do that when you suffered from PTSD. If you can remember you let me do the same when I suffered from PTSD. All we both needed was that someone who was willing to take the time to just listen to the painful memories going through our head and heart.

He wants to talk about it, but he doesn't have anyone who cares enough to want to listen to him. It's having that person who shows he is ready to listen. Let him cry. Let him cry until there are no more tears left to cry. The cry is the physical release of that mental torment he's going through."

"Val, how you know all this?" "I've had friends that went through this same situation after being medivac. When I was at Madigan at Fort Lewis, when I got medevac back from Iraq.

I had a close friend who had a very close battle buddy who got killed and he died in his arms. He told me about how he took his hands trying to keep his battle buddy's inside together and holding it in hoping the medic could save him.

He was injured and they sent him back to Madigan. He was Hispanic and we became very close friends. He told me the story of how they were on a door to door search. An IED went off as they went through the door. His battle buddy fell back on him. He said that's probably what saved him.

He kept saying in tears he called for medic but he was already dead. He was trying to hold he guts in but the blood kept coming out. As he told me the story he was acting out what he was doing at that time. He kept saying SARG, I couldn't do nothing to help my battle. All I could do was hold him and cry. I was wounded but I didn't want to let him go.

All he could hear was him friend say, "Ah shit man I'm dead." He said I kept saying no man you going be alright, I got you. But it was too late. He said he felt so guilty. My friend's name was Specialist Gonzales.

One day we was working a puzzle in the day room, I asked him why he feel so guilty. He said we both should have died. Then I wouldn't feel so bad. When I left to come home on convalescence he was still there.

I never forgot what he told me. He said SFC I've never been able to talk about what happened to my battle buddy over there. It still hurts but I feel better since I cried and let it out I feel better. Now I can call my family and maybe one day Corporal Pierce's too. He told me he had been there for three months and never called his family. I've never heard from him again.

That's when I though back when Chaplain Herring told me, who was my pastor back in Los Angeles, told me "Maybe it is time for you to go home. You are hurt and some people refused to see that, when we refuses to do things that are for our best interest.

God makes that way for it to happen. It is time for you to go home. Keep in mind war brings the worse out in good people. Especially in those who you think got your back." I've never forgotten those words".

I've had several friends come back and go berserk at work because they don't talk about what the experience in combat or in a combat zone. It doesn't have to be a person getting injured or killed.

It could be some very overly zealous individuals in charge trying to push his weight around to some lower ranking individual. There was a lot of that when I was deployed to Kuwait. People who were trying to make a name for themselves through the tormenting of a fellow soldier.

Leadership abuse was a big thing there. People you thought would have your back would stab you in your back. They would do some of the most inhuman things to their fellow soldiers and to their once friends. I even had that happened to me.

As you should know deployment brings out the worse in those whom you looked up to as your leaders. I saw that with my own eyes. I say all that to say, anxiety, has a lot to do with what happens to an individual while deployed. Most of the times you don't know you have PTSD or whatever.

Even though they try to screen it when you redeploy. Then all of a sudden something happens and set you off. Like a bus driver beating a customer because he asked a simple question.

The mind just snaps, anxiety and anticipation kick in and you lose it. Most would call it PTSD. But, before Post Traumatic Stress Disorder came about, soldier returning from deployment. Most was diagnosis with a condition known as "Instability Complex" where an individual has an uncertainty or unsure how to handle a current situation which has led to a form of aggression or anger.

A lot of homeless has this same condition but society has labeled it PTSD. Many with this have been placed and ends up in mental institution. When if the individual situation has changed it's a possibility the condition would change for the better. Then you come back and face some very bad things that can set a person off like Jim.

So, what y'all going to do about Jim?" "What did you say to him when you got there?" "When I got there I ask him what's going on. You sound quite upset on the phone." "He said he was but he didn't know where to begin." Why don't you begin from the beginning that's always a good place to start?" Just as he began to tell me Chief walked in and we started over again. I told Chief, Jim was about to tell what's been going on with him.

Daniel said, Chief replied yeah Jim-bow I been worried about you, man. We've been very concerned about you. I wasn't sure how to ask you then you called and you sound very upset. So what's going on buddy?" "Like I was about to tell CSM. When you dropped me off in LA. I wasn't sure where to get any information. I contacted a buddy of mine's who was on the LA police department.

I told what had happened and he said he'll do some checking on it for me. He suggested that I go by the university and ask the security over there. Well, I did and they weren't any help.

I contacted Anna and she gave me some girl by the name of Kathy and where she may live up in the North Hollywood area. I got a copy of a school photo from the security and made some missing person flyers and posted them in area where I was told college kids hung out at fraternity and Sorority houses. I went around to them asking have they seen her and they all said no.

I was told it's a possibility she may be up in the Hollywood area a lot of college kids hang out there on weekends. I went to the address Anna had and they told me nobody live there by that name. I spent weeks trying to locate a lead that may give me something.

I went back to my hotel and there was a message about a possible lead that a man had left for me. The message said for me to meet him at a clinic in Hollywood. I went up to the place which was supposed to be a clinic, but it wasn't a clinic. It was more like a rundown boarding house. I went in there and the person told me to go down to some place a few block away. That's where the clinic was.

I went in there and that's where they told me women come here all the time but if I had a picture they would contact me if she showed up. I left the picture of Stephanie at the desk and they assured me they would contact me. This was about two weeks into my search for Stephanie.

About a week later just waiting around waiting for a call I finally got a call. I had almost given up and ready to come back home. Well, the call said they had some information and if I go back the first address I had went to up in Hollywood they may have some information that could lead to the location of Stephanie.

Well I went there and that where I ran into some very unfriendly guys. They were three guys big bouncer type. The first one hit me as I walked in the door and I fell to my knees. They took turn beating until I was too weak to fight back. They told me stop asking question or they will make sure I won't ask another one.

They kept asking me who sent you. What agency are you with. I kept telling them I'm trying to find my daughter. You don't have no daughter. That's the last thing I heard before something sharp like a needle went through my arm. Someone said he's not out yet give him another shot. That's was when I got sick to my stomach.

That's when I heard a woman said you fools you're going to kill him before I get the extraction. I need his body warm you fools. See if you can bring him around so we can remove the organ. He looks very healthy we might can get two from him. That's when I tried to fight back again. They knock me out again. I woke a little groggy but I felt like I was moving. I felt a deep pain in my side.

The vehicle stopped and I was carried in a rundown building from the back, up some stairs. I heard a voice say that's the man they looking for. I felt my body sitting or maybe lying on a lot of ice cold water and I fell to sleep went unconscious again.

I just kept feeling all this coldness around me and I couldn't get up. I was in a lot of pain and unfamiliar voices I kept hearing. The last thing I remember I think your voice CSM asking is he alive. That's when I knew I was safe.

I went through this and I didn't accomplish a single thing. I didn't find a bit of information about my daughter missing. I end up almost dead by someone needing my kidney. All I wanted to do was find my daughter.

Now I've got all this going on in my life and I don't know where to even start to fix it. I'm not like you guys I don't have what you have to get things done when it needs to be done. I screwed up the only chance to find my daughter and now I can't help her after you guys go out and save her when it should have been me.

This thing has got me all twisted in the head Chief I don't know which way to turn." "That's why we're here now Jim. We're going to try and do this thing together." He started to cry "I don't know what to do I feel like I just want to die"

"Come on Jim you can't be saying things like that you know we can't have you dying on us. You're the next one on the triangle. We've been through too much together. We're going to get through this together. Go home get some rest and we'll meet at the mansion tomorrow and set down and figure this out.

Now you got to promise us Jim you're not going to do anything foolish like kill yourself. Just remember there is always an answer to every situation. You just got to find it. Promise me Jim."

"Jimbo I just want you to know. When we couldn't find you that was the most difficult times I had to go through not knowing whether you were dead or alive. I kept praying and believing that you weren't. When that guy said you were alive, all I could say was thank you God."

"I never knew y'all were looking for me until I woke up in the hospital. By then I was too embarrassed and too disappointed in myself. Knowing I had wasted all this time and hadn't accomplished anything. By then I didn't know what to do. I hadn't expected to be gone that long maybe a day or two if I had come up with some leads. I kept telling myself something was going to break. It never happened."

"Jim why didn't you call one of us? If we had known. You know we would have been right there just like tonight. When one of us is troubled we took a solemn oath to always be there for each other. When one of us is in trouble or needs help we are there for each other. Come on Jim I thought you knew that. I know we've had our spats but we always managed to work it out after we kind of gave each other space. It has never gotten this far."

"I know I guess I was being somewhat prideful doing this whole ordeal. I don't know how I let it get this far to the point I don't know what to do. I don't know where my head was. I couldn't think, I was making wrong decision or just none at all. I had no idea where I was heading."

"Well Jim-bob we're here now. We're going to set down tomorrow and try to figure this thing out that you're going through. I think we have an idea but, we're going to put our heads together as we should have done, and we've done in the past. Keep in minds guys nothing is too big or too small that we don't have each other's back. Just remember guys each of us is that connecting point to that three sided triangle the makes up HIE. If one is broke or lost it affects the hold group. A lot of people depend on us so we must depend on each other."

"So, honey, that's pretty much what happened and what we decided on and where we are now. I have to admit out of the almost twenty years this company been together. I've never looked at HIE that way. I never thought of the triangle came up to what Chief said. The triangle represents the three of us.

When one is broke or lost it affects all of us and even though I'm not there anymore, in a leadership position, I am a part of the triangle." "Daniel, who're you trying to fool? You know you will always play a part in what HIE get involve in. You might be retired, but I know Chief fills you in on almost everything that goes on at the company.

I don't understand, why didn't he tell you about Jim going to look for his daughter?" "I don't think he knew he was still gone. Jim was spending time at home with Charmaine since they found out they were having twins. Chief did some calling around that's when we decided we need to go check it out. That was about almost two weeks since he left.

We had Eloise do up some flyer with a five thousand dollar reward just for information that might lead to finding him. That was to spark some interest in keeping a look out for him. We had a lot of leads but most of them lead to a dead end. Until, that cleaning woman called and that's mainly because she wanted the reward. That's what lead us to Jim.

No one would help us they thought we were the FBI. I think whoever did what they did to him had intended to leave him there to die. Like so many others. I think Jim was getting too close and they felt they had to get rid of him. So they found a way to get rid of him and make a profit.

Don't you know that human organ is the highest commodity in the world? A kidney can go for up to a million dollars depends on how bad they need one and as low as two hundred thousand dollars.

Lord only knows what the going price for a heart or lung, which all ends in death for the donor. Sad to say only the rich and famous can afford these organs and families ends up finding a healthy family member dead of some unknown cause.

During our investigation we learned though Los Angeles corners and the FBI they have long lists of unidentified corpse with missing organs but with unknown causes of death. Their biggest questions are where and how they found these bodies. And of course skid row is the biggest dumping ground for these bodies and corpses. Most were very healthy unwilling donors.

We may never find who did this to Jim but I bet you any amount of money somehow it all ties into the abduction, human trafficking, phony adoptions and sex trade. Let's get some sleep. I have a busy day in the morning." "Daniel." "Yeah, honey" "I'm glad you and Jim manage to work out your differences. I can sleep better knowing this." "Me too honey, Now go to sleep, its late."

CHAPTER
Three

We later found out Jim was not suffering from PTSD even though he did go through a very traumatic experience. He was very fortunate considering the beating he received and the drugs they gave him to keep him alive for the removal of his kidney.

Daniel said he was diagnosis with what is called "Instability Complex". A condition most soldiers get from redeployment. It is commonly confused with PTSD. The individual become uncertain in how to handle normal everyday situations. They become somewhat agitated, aggressive and quickly angered. All these symptoms are what Jim had. He was never a real threat to anyone but his own frame of mind.

He had to learn how to focus on each situation. Break it down in detail for him to handle and understand what the problem or situation that just occurred. It didn't take Jim long to be his old self again.

That made Soup really happy. It changed his relationship with the rest of the team and the COC. Things eventually worked out between the three, which made me very happy. I didn't ask but I really wanted to know the rest of that story. Maybe one day he'll tell me.

Jim now having a pretty good relationship with Stephanie who went back to college but in Texas. She wanted to work on her relationship with her father.

Thinking back at what we found out in reference to Stephanie incident when she was going to USC. She had become a victim of a group rape at one of the fraternity parties. This had come out during one of her sessions with Chaplain Anderson. Although Daniel had his own people investigating the situation that lead to Stephanie abduction.

She had gone to a Frat party with her new found friend which she called Kathy. She told her she think she was pregnant and she wanted to get an abortion. Kathy told her she knew of an abortion clinic up in Hollywood where some other students went to have an abortion.

Stephanie told her mother she was going to a party up in Hollywood with her friend Kathy and she was going to spend the night at her place. Kathy took her to the place where the physician informed her she was too far gone to have an abortion. She was told if she didn't want the child she could put it up for adoption. They told her she was almost three months pregnant. The clinic had a connection with an adoption agency that place babies in very good prominent homes. All she had to do is sign the papers and when the child is delivered the child would go to a very good couple wanting a baby.

She said she agreed to the abortion counselor advice because she was too young to have to worry about a child because she saw what her mother went through with her. She had other plans and she was raped and she did want no "Rape Baby".

Plus she had no idea who was the father of the baby. The counselor told her she would be taken by one of the aids to the lawyer's office to sign the forfeit of the child because of the circumstances the child was conceived. She said she agreed to it. She was driven by a lady and two men to the Anaheim's Airport where she was directed to get on the flight with three other young girls who look almost, if not more, pregnant as her.

She asked where they were taking them. To a place where she would be comfortable until she delivered the baby. She told them she had to go home her mother would be worried about her and would call the police.

The woman told her she should have thought of that before she had sex with five guys at a FRAT party. She started screaming I was raped. The woman told her you may have been raped but you are now pregnant and that baby you are carrying no longer is your baby. You signed papers to give that child up for adoption. So you need to behave or you and your baby will not live to see another day. Do I make myself clear?

So they took her to a place where she shared a room with four other girls more pregnant then she was. She was separated from the three girls she came there with. Every time one girl left to deliver her child they would put another girl in the room. One of the girls died because she was hemorrhaging and the baby was still born. It was offal. Someone told me they threw both of them in the ocean. I was told once they have their baby they are placed in prostitution. Some never make it that far.

We were always watched by other women who took turns taking care of us. If we disobey them they would hold back our food so we couldn't eat for days. This was a very dark room with no windows. We could not talk to each other. If they caught us talking they would make us stand for hours. Our legs would ache from the pain and the baby. The women who were in charge of us were mainly Asian. We called them all Mama-sung they did not have names we could call them by. Sometimes they were nice but most of the time they would call us names in their language and push us if we didn't understand them.

When I went in labor two of them took me in a room in the back. When my baby was born they were yelling the word Negro. Which meant black. I heard one say it's a boy and they went and got one of the other women in charged.

They took the baby and wrapped him up and I never say him. I was then placed in a room with other girls who just gave birth. I was told after I heal I will be going home. But one of the other girls who were a prostitute told me that's what they told her but, they made me a prostitute somewhere in one of the Broth houses in Asia where she was sold.

She said if her family could find her they would buy her back. She left two days later I never saw her again. About maybe a week later, I was taken to a place where I was given an examination to see if I had any type of what they called female disease before they sold me. They took pictures of me doing all kind of different poses. A couple of them were having sex with women and men. I got sick at the stomach but I blank it out my mind.

Then one day they took me out of the place I was in and carried me to a boat where there were a lot of men with guns watching over us. They took us to an island I think where they gave us a new name and told us when they called that name they want us to go out and show them all the poses that we were showed to do in front of the camera.

I went out and did the poses I was taught. I think that's when a man told me to go get ready to leave I was going to a new place.

I started to cry until I heard a voice say Stephanie. I really started to cry then. That meant somebody knew me as Stephanie. They took me to this warehouse where there was a Chinese man and two African American men dressed as if they were from Africa.

The Chinese man said my name is Col Woo. This is Chief and CSM they've come to take you home. I ran to hug them. I think I tripped. One of them caught me and said you're safe now. Your ride is waiting to take you home.

I think I cried most of the way. The guys who was bringing me home was so good to me. They treated with so much kindness something I hadn't known for almost over a year. JT told me we have a surprise for you once we land.

After about six months of therapy Stephanie was able to talk about her ordeal.

Daniel's team he had investigating the abduction was able to come up with pictures of the young lady who befriended Stephanie, in which she identified her.

COL Woo's associates with Polaris contacted the authorities which lead them to the individuals who ran the phony abortion clinic in Hollywood and arrested several of the people running the clinic and the phony baby adoption scam.

Daniel said some of the people got away who was involved in the scam, but they did make arrest of the so called doctors and lawyers involved in the scams. It took Daniel's teams about six months to assist in the exposure of those involved in the scam and the abduction.

The guys involved in the "Frat Rape Train" pulled on Stephanie was never all identified. But with Little Jim's DNA his father was identified. One morning, Daniel called Chief and told him they had some unfinished business in Lovett, TX.

Daniel filled Chief in on it in route up to Lovett. Chief told Daniel, I been your back up for a very long time. I'll take the lead. Let me do this.

I've got a god son at home that means the world to me and Eloise; and I owe him as well as Stephanie the pleasure of putting these scum bags where they belong beginning with Mr. Big Oil Baron.

Daniel said Chief walked in to that Oil Baron office in the middle of one of his big meetings with his associates.

Chief said you might not know me but I know you and that rapist of a son very well. I've got one thing to say. As he dropped on the table a copy of the DNA proof of the son being the legitimate father of Little Jim.

Your son is the father of my god son. I want you to know what kind of son you have raised and allowed to run wild in this world. He and a group of his frat brother ran a "Rape Train" on my god-son's mother.

She had gone through a traumatic experience in these past years because of what they did to her. Which I will not go in detail about it.

I want you to know Little Jim doesn't want or need anything from you or your son to rectify what he has put this young lady and her son through.

I just want you to know who I am and what I am capable of doing without a doubt in my mind or heart. I am part owner of HIE, LLC the largest explosive experts in this part of the world.

I'm pretty sure you have heard of us. I said this to let you know, you and your son owe my god-son collateral damage for what you put them both through. I expect to hear from you both in the very near future.

Just to make sure you understand where I am coming from. I have just as much money as you have and maybe more but, I've got more firepower than you can come up with your lawyers.

This sir is no threat. This is a promise. I have enough firepower in my stockade to blow up every oil field you own. What I can't complete my brother CSM will finish. Oh, by the way they call me Chief. I hope to hear from you both very soon.

Daniel said Chief walked out that office madder than he has ever seen him. Two days later the big old baron and his spawn showed up at HIE, LLC with three of their lawyers trying to work out a deal.

Chief still mad as hell, called three of our lawyers and they worked a deal. Where Stephanie and Little Jim would never have a need for anything the rest of their lives. It took Chief a good while to get over the situation. Daniel said I'm glad I've never been on his bad side.

I told him you are two of a kind. I can tell you two are brothers. You sure you not twins? It runs in the family. You were going to blow up a country and he was going to blow up a town and oil fields. Yeah, you are two of a kind.

A month later Daniel got a call from one of his buddies up in DC. "I heard something about you and Chief bulldozed your way into one of the oil baron office in Texas and threated to blow them up." He said, "Yes we did, and that was not a threat. If I can remember, it was a promise. One we were going to keep. That's nothing compared to what they would have done to one of us if we had did what that son of his and his frat buddies did. I'll leave it at that.

Now is that what you called me for or is there something else you want to discuss." He said, "No, I just wanted to hear your side. I know you brothers don't just put out idle threats. Unless there are very good reasons." "Believe me it was a very good reason." "Ok man, keep in touch." He said that was the end of that.

CHAPTER Four

After that we decided to spend more time at the beach house away from all the business in HIE. For the past two years I enjoyed our get-aways together to the beach house. Where I could just relax and think about how fortunate I was and the life I have. I often thought back to my time growing up on the hill on Short Eighth Street.

As I laid back with my eyes half closed feeling the breeze and the morning sun on my face. I could hear Daniel trying to sneak up, as the crew made their easy growl, letting me know he was there. He sat in the chair next to me and said, "You look very relaxed." "I am." "What you thinking about?" "I was just thinking, when I was growing up and how Janelle treated her grandmother the way she did when she was growing up.

I can remember my grandmother continuity of raising me and my three sisters even after our mother died. We were her priority as she and the family struggled trying to raise us back then. I can remember how hard it was for her, my two uncles and aunt working together raising us kids.

They had kids of their own, but they all pulled together to raising us." "How were you raised and grew up for that matter? You've never really talked about how you were raised." "We were a very close family. We were like a clan, my grandmother being matriarch of the family or clan for that matter.

I was raised in a small college town in Virginia, called Charlottesville, nestled between the well-known Walton Mountain and the Monticello Mountain (home of Thomas Jefferson) is where I grew up. Growing up, we lived on a hard gravel road called Short Eighth Street, near the Eighth Street railroad tunnel under path. There were six houses on the hill where we lived. The Luck Family, Miller family, Uncle Chuck and his family, Mama's house, Brother's house and his family, and Miss Mattie and her son and family. Many called us poor, but now, I see it as just not having a lot.

Growing up we were known as those poor little kids that lived on the Road. We lived in the house with our grandmother and her two daughters. Her name was Mittie and her daughters' names were Alice and Mary. She also had two sons Walton and Linwood. They each had children and families of their own. My mother, Alice, (the youngest of the four) whom we called "Elise" had four girls, me and my three sisters.

My Aunt Mary (next to the oldest), whom we called Sister, had two girls who lived with us in Mama's house. Walton (the oldest son) whom we all called Brother, had the spirit and a loving calm soul of mama. He was a very quiet and peace loving man dedicated to his mama and wife who were sickly with breast cancer. They had a daughter who was a nurse and had three girls and a boy.

Then there was Linwood next to the youngest, who they called Babe boy. He was the most aggressive of the four siblings. We had the understanding he was most like his father whereas, Brother was more like his mother, Mama. Uncle Chuck, which we kids called him, was married with five kids, (three boys and two girls).

We were a very close and loving family whom all lived on that hill on Short Eighth Street with Mama as the matriarch of the family. She was very much loved and highly respected by everyone who lived on that gravel road. This was mainly because of her strength, and loving kindness towards everyone that lived on the road. Even though we did not have a lot, we were a proud family. Each of mama's children were hard working individuals and who went to work every day to help support and provide for their families.

Those were hard times back then growing up on the hill. Mama, the matriarch of the family was the disciplinary of the family. It was nothing for her to skin a keen switch off one of the bushes in the yard and tan our leg or behind if we were sassy or disrespectful to any grownup.

Disrespect to a grownup was not tolerated in her house. If there were any grownups' presence, we were to always answer with a yes ma'am or yes sir. We were not allowed to answer a grownup with a plain yes or no. When grownups were talking among themselves, she would send us out from their presence. She believed young folk had no business getting in or listening to grown folk conversations.

In spite of her strict disciplinary ways, she had the best hugs and kisses in the world with the compassion of Mother Theresa. She could ease the pain and hurt by the sound of her voice or the touch of her hand. Her love poured out whenever she spoke a kind word or did a kind jester. She would never say a mean or bad thing about anyone, no matter how bad or bitter the person was. She did not believe in gossiping or listening to any ill will about anyone. She just believed everyone has a reason for doing what they do or say. Even though mama couldn't read or write she was one of the smartest people I have ever known. To this day I still feel her kindred spirit around me."

As I spoke my eyes began to tear as I spoke of Mama; I then continued, "Along with her heart filled wisdom, kindness, and knowledge of understanding, she had an undying love for God and instilled that love of God in each of us by constantly giving him praise. Words like "Praise the Lord", "thank you Jesus", "Lord have mercy" and always asking God for his blessings, mercy and his forgiveness for us.

Mama believed when the Lord is doing his work, in other words when a storm is going on, we should be very quiet and still. She would bring us all in one room, cut all the lights off, pull all the shades down and have us sit very still in the house until the storm was over. Most of the time we kids end up falling to sleep.

At mealtime, meant the whole family would all set down at the dinner table together. Each of us would take turn saying the blessing giving thanks to the Lord God for our meal, no matter how big or small our meal, we were eating. After our meal we would asked to be excused from the table and took our dirty dish with us.

We all went to bed around the same time, (I image because Sister and Elise had to be at work before dawn at the hospital) as we lay in bed, mama would lead us in our nightly ritual, the "Lord's Prayer" and we would repeat after her. She would pray for the rich and the poor, the sick and the flicked, in each and every hospital all over the world. She would always ask God to bless all eight of us by name. Sister's youngest daughter sometimes during the night would wake up hollowing because she used to have bad nightmare. She would wake up everybody in that one upstairs bedroom. Sister would have to shake her and make her go back to sleep.

Growing up I guess I was somewhat of a very mischievous child. I remember I got one of the worse spankings from my grandmother when I frighten my cousin really bad and made her cry. I was hiding behind the door which separates the kitchen from the living room. I jumped from behind the door growling like a bear. Frances started yelling and screaming running back into the kitchen.

Mama grabbed me by my arm and gave me a bad spanking with her hand. To this day I still remember the pain my butt felt after that spanking. Mama said, "I told y'all children about scaring that girl, you know she has nightmare at night." We didn't care it was funny to us. I couldn't go outside for the rest of the day. Although we used to pick on our cousin Frances a lot when growing up, we did not let anyone outside the family mess with her; not even our mean cousins that lived with Uncle Chuck. I would fight anybody who did.

I was always known as the fighter in the family when I was little. I've been told, I took that after my mom; she was somewhat of a tomboy and a fighter. She was playing ball on the road the day she went in labor having me. I was born at home almost on the front steps. My grandmother delivered me on one of the hottest days in July as my Uncle Chuck told me one day we were talking during my teenage years. He told me they were all in the road playing ball and she went into labor and almost had the baby on the steps. They called the ambulance, but they took so long, so the baby was coming so fast Mama delivered me on the sofa in the living room. I guess that's why I was so close to my grandmother.

I was the youngest of us three girls and very much spoiled by Mama, until Glo, the baby came along. I was always somewhat of a dreamer and a wonderer. As I grew older, I would wonder off and get in more trouble than anyone person could find in that wooded area behind the house where we lived (which we called the jungles).

I loved climbing the apple, pear and walnut trees in the field behind our house, swinging on the long swinging vines in the jungles, (imaging I was Jane in Tarzan) and chasing butterflies through the field. In my world, this was my paradise growing up.

I knew every spot and hiding place throughout that jungle from our backyard to the path where the old drunks and winos hung out near the railroad track where I loved to play along those tracks that lead to Miss Mattie's the bootlegger's house.

I would get lost in my dreaming and imagination when I was in that field until I heard mama's voice calling me to come home. Hanging out in that jungle, and running through those bushes barefoot and climbing trees, mama had cured my many bouts with poison oak, sticker brayer, and pine needle on my body.

She would say, "Girrl you better stay out of that field before you get bit by one of those snakes or catch poison oak". In the summertime I loved walking barefoot in the soft grass in our back yard up on the hill. My favorite past time was laying in the grass watching the puffy clouds and airplanes passing overhead leaving trails of smoke in the bright blue sky. I knew one day I would ride in one.

Holidays on the hill was a lot of fun we often celebrate with our cousins on Brother's side. Uncle Chuck's wife never let her kids come out to play with us only once in a while. We didn't care because we had fun with our cousins on Brother's side of the family. Uncle Chuck's kids were mean especially the boys. They would always pick on Sister's daughter Frances and usually that meant we would end up fussing with them. I asked Mama one time why Uncle Chuck's wife wouldn't let the kids come out and play.

She would say, she didn't know. I guess she had her reasons and left it at that. Many times they would be at the window watching us play in the back yard or on the gravel road in the front yard playing. I felt sorry for them but then when they came outside the boys would take our toys and hit on us. I would always fight them back and Mama would make me come in the house and set in the kitchen. She would tell me I should not fight people because they don't know any better. I didn't care I would fight them anyway.

When Halloween came around, Mama did not allow us to go trick or treat, because there were many white people who did mean and hateful things to colored people during those times. She made sure we had our own celebration. Brother and Sister would buy Halloween candy, corn candy, ginger snaps and lemon snap cookies, and apples. Mama had gotten fruits from the produce man who came by the house, for our party. We would each get a bag of goodies and we would play like we were trick or treating at our two houses on the hill.

When wintertime came that's when the chicken man would bring the live chickens and we had to pluck the feathers off them. Mr. Shifflet would bring the live chickens in a cage and he would pick them out for Mama. He would cut their head off and they would run around the back yard with their heads cut off and until they fell down dead. I guess that's where the saying came from, "Stop, running around like a chicken with his head cut off." I did not like when they did that.

I used to be so scared of those headless chicken running around the yard. Afterward, Mama would have a tub of boiling water to soak them in so we could pluck their feathers out of them. Wet chickens was the worse smelling thing you could smell. Mama cooked every part of the chicken even the chicken feet. She used to get hog head from the chicken man with their eyes still in them and their snort or nose still on them. She brought every part of the hog and pig from his head to his feet, and she cooked every part of them also.

Thanksgiving is when Mama cooked the best baked macaroni and cheese casserole in the world. She would make the best yellow pound cakes and apple and sweet potatoes pies from scratch. She would have us pluck string beans where she would throw in a ham hock to give it flavor. Mama would cook enough food to feed both families for days. We would all set down at the table and Mama would lead us in grace. We all ate until we couldn't eat anymore.

Our Christmas on the hill, Mama made Christmas the best she could. She was never one to borrow money for such things. She would always make do with what we had. She would make cakes and pies from scratch. She would store them in the wooden icebox on the back porch. I can remember helping her in the kitchen putting sliced apples in the pie shells and stirring the batter for the cakes.

She would let me eat the batter and the frosting she made from chocolate "coco" powder mix left in the mixing bowls. She would take food coloring and make us different color cupcakes and icing on the cakes. She would make sweet potato pies and banana pudding with homemade whip cream on top. Mama would start baking her cakes and pies days before Christmas and store them with wax paper over them in the wooden Icebox on the back porch.

We never got a lot of toys for Christmas. She made sure we got at least one toy we asked Santa Claus for and one new outfit for Christmas. I remember my aunt took us to Sears Roebuck to see Santa Clause. I was scared to death. I ran all through that store they had to drag me up to him. We each would put an old sock up around the mantel piece for Santa to fill the stocking. We were so anxious. Sleep did not come so easy that time of year. We could not wait to wake up Christmas morning.

As Children, our hopes were all so high that time of season. We would be so excited on Christmas Eve night we could hardly go to sleep. Mama would make us go to bed at our usual nine o'clock time. We kids would lie in bed and talk about what we wanted Santa to bring us until Mama would hollow up the stairs and say "You children need to be quite and go to sleep." So we would close our eyes and eventually drift off to sleep.

We had many very deep snowy Christmases on the hill. I remember early one Christmas morning; we were awoken by a voice out on the road saying, "HO! HO! HO! Merry Christmas." I could have sworn to this day that voice was Santa Claus. My aunt told us, you children lay back down that's just somebody going down the road.

Mama knew how excited we kids were; and we would wake up early lying in bed whispering among ourselves. We could smell the fatback bacon and biscuit cooking downstairs. Mama would call upstairs and tell us come see what Santa brought us.

We would come running downstairs, running from place to place looking for our Christmas gifts. Now, the custom was then, you leave an old toy for Santa and he would exchange it for a new one. When we came downstairs there would be brown paper lunch sack with our names on them filled with apples, oranges, tangerines and lots of hard candy sitting next to our Christmas toy and our new outfit from Santa. We were so sure Santa had come the night before and left all the gifts for us. We would be so happy although we never really got the toy we wished for, but the one Santa wanted us to have. Sometimes that was ok.

The house would smell of turkey, ham, cinnamon, and vanilla from the pies and cakes which Mama had worked so hard to finish before they came to bed. We would all set down to a big breakfast, of Ho-cake biscuits, dripping in butter and dark Karol maple Syrup, soft scrambled eggs and crispy fatback salt bacon. Afterward we would play with our new toys and eat as much as our stomach could hold. Later that day Mama would call us to supper and we would all sit at the table together and say the blessing together. Mama would let us eat until we were too full to eat anymore.

After supper we kids would put on our Christmas play we had practice so hard for. We would have on costumes we had made for the performance. We would sing Christmas songs and dance our little parts for the family. Afterward we would all sit on the floor in front of the black and white TV and watch the Christmas programs until it was time for bed. We kids would go to bed and talk among ourselves about the day until mama them came up for bed, and we all said the Lord's Prayer together and prayed for everyone.

I loved the beautiful signs of spring on the hill. When just at the crack of dawn, the waking sound of birds chirping in nearby trees, signaling spring is here it's time to get up. The beauty of dogwood trees blossoming along the bank with flowers of pink and white, and the blossom of every fruit that grew in the meadows and along each vine.

I relish the sweet smell of morning glories clinging to honeysuckle vine along the fence in the meadows and fields. While on the hill behind the house are filled with my favorite yellow and orange Snap Dragons; and where Queen Anne Lace flowers grew wild blowing softly in the morning breeze.

Every Easter Mama would have Sister take us girls down to Robinson Department store to buy us new dresses. She would buy us new shoes from Miss Tilly, a Jewish woman where she would let Mama buy us shoes on what she called time. Miss Tilly and Mama had been friends for years. She knew all us children by name and would always take time to wait on us making sure we got the right shoe and size. She called Mama, Miss Mittie. She showed so much respect for our grandmother.

So, Mama would make sure we would get a new dress and pair shoes for Easter to wear to Sunday school and church. She would have Sister braid our hair in three braids, one big braid on top and one on each side in the back, each braid had a bow ribbon to match our dress. We looked so pretty.

Mama made sure we went to Sunday school. She was a member of Zion Union Baptist Church with Rev Kenny as the pastor. After Church Mama would have boiled eggs and dyed them for us to hide in the back yard up on the hill. We kids and Brother's grandchildren would have an Easter egg hunt after church with jelly beans and little yellow marshmallow peep candy chicks to eat.

Summers came and summers went. The school year always started in September. We were all excited about going back to school the first few weeks. All us kids would get a new outfit to wear on that first day of the school year. She brought us each school shoes, black and white saddle bags oxford, from Miss Tilly and her brothers; and clothes from Robinson department store.

The rest of the year we would wear hand me down or used clothes given to us by people Mama would do the wash for. Shoes, we were the hardest on us. Sometimes we would wear shoes with newspaper or soft cardboard (we would eventually wear the cardboard out too) in the bottom of them because of the holes we had worn in the soles. Many would say we were poor, but we didn't know any better. In Mama's eyes and in her heart we just didn't have a lot, like others would have.

Many at that time didn't have a lot. Some would have called that a form of poverty, but in reality, being poor or poverty is all just a form of mindset. As I think more and more about Mama, all she wanted was to take care of her four little grandchildren who lost their mother and her baby daughter to a very bad disease, "Leukemia". She knew of no status quo or paid any attention to what people may have said.

We were happy and we were grateful. As a child I loved those times (living on that hill and that hard gravel road) realizing we weren't poor, we just didn't have a lot.

But knowing, what we did have was a lot of love in a family that loved each other so very much. Mama struggled to raise us children but, she loved each of us the same and, she let each of us know that.

Even though life for us was a struggle but, we kids didn't notice it as a struggle. Many could say we were poor, but we didn't know any better. Maybe we didn't have a lot but, in Mama's eyes and in her heart we did have a lot. We had each other's love and compassion that radiated from our grandmother's heart she showed to each of us through her loving and caring for her family.

If I asked her that question today knowing her she would say, they weren't talking about how rich or how poor we were. Everyone was struggling and going through hard times but most didn't notice they were living and making do with what they had as mama and her family did.

One time I asked mama is we poor. She said, "No babe they were just feeling sorry for you four girls because your mother had died. The Lord has blessed you children with a mother who worked all her life to take care of you children and when the Lord called her home she made sure you were taken care and you all are so blessed. No they were speaking of you poor four little girls who lost your mother to that deadly disease called "Leukemia."

"Val, you were very blessed growing up. I have to say you are very candid when you speak of your childhood. I would love to hear more about your life growing up," Daniel said, as he sat there focusing on every word I said.

"That's because I had nothing to be embarrassed of, it was hard during those times and Mama took away my deepest fear." "What fear was that?" "That one day they would come and take us girls away from mama them, but she made sure that never happened. My mother worked hard and when she died, mama got a check every month from her social security to take care of her girls. Yes we were very blessed."

"So Val, was your mother sick for a long time?" "The strange thing about that, us children didn't really know or should I say noticed that. You know during those times grown folks kept that kind of stuff away from the children until it happens and then just like my grandmother did, told us when the time came and the passing.

She sheltered us from many things growing up. Especially things that she felt would harm us. But, as a child all we did was eat, play and sleep. As for me, and getting into mischief on the hill. She even sheltered us from what people may have thought of us as a clan living on that hill. We were known as those Chisholm's.

We all had to eventually move off that hill by the railroad tracks and was placed in temporary housing by the government and because the government was making that area into the city's first government housing projects. They called it "The West Haven Housing Project".

This was where I grew up fast but loved the life I lived in the Projects. People was place there from all parts of the city's slums and rundown residences. I met and found some of my closest friends and my first real boyfriend. The tomboy in me became a strong willed young woman. I played soft ball on the neighborhood team and was a very tough right fielder.

This is when I realized I did not want to be like some of the girlfriends I had grew up with. I did not want to be like them with kids by different guys at a very young age. After going through what I thought with love, I had been given a chance to change my life unknowing this is not what God had in store for me.

I wanted to fulfill my dream by joining the military and travel. Maybe someday ride in a big airplane. My destiny had changed just by me taking the chance to make a change in my life as a soldier. After marrying a man that took us both to the other side of the country and the world. I became that person I had wanted to be and see things I'd only imagine of but, always wanted to see and do.

Now as we gathered at the summer house for our second Fourth of July celebration with family and extended family. Those we have met through the years of our many celebrations. The company has grown by two more teams one in Germany and the other in Hawaii. I never could understand why they needed a team in Germany. His explanation these were just satellite teams to pick up the slack once the final drawdowns began. Chief said there probable never be another drawdown considering the change in our country's leadership and weaponry. They were beginning to train their teams in Hawaii and at the sites up in Wisconsin.

Chief, Eloise, Sport and Chaplain Anderson flew in early. Tom was coming in later he had some unfinished business he wanted to complete before the long weekend. Jai and Soup came in early and sent her pilot in the company's larger Jet to pick up Jim and his family and Stephanie. They stopped and picked up DJ and his family at Fort Hood. The family were beginning to assemble at the summer house. Daniel and Chief said since the family was growing so fast and big they needed a larger jet to just transport the family.

We all assemble around the open barbeque pit as we decided who were staying where. We did not want to do the assigning who was staying where. Daniels, after announcing, "We now have two CSMs in the family, DJ had just been promoted to CSM." He raised he glass and toasted, "To the new and junior, (as he winked to salute to) Commander Sergeant Major Daniel J. Howard III my hero."

He then politely said, "Your first duty as the junior CSM in the family is to assign sleeping quarters for the rest of the family. Just

LOVE, LIFE'S ENDLESS DESTINY

keep in mind son we are all here on a family retreat vacation. This is a directive no business is allowed these next three days." They all cheered.

DJ assigned everyone where they were going to sleep. Cory and Courtney who was the oldest of the young ones decided they would be in charge of the young ones. They had come up with activities to keep the younger kids busy. DJ said, "I figure you two could do a better job that I could with you two." Courtney said, "You were so bossy. We see hasn't much changed." He said, "Well, at least I get paid for it and I get no complaints." Cory said, "Yes, CSM". Daniel walked over and asked, "Well, son how it feel being a Command Sergeant Major?" "I don't know pops. It feels kind of strange. I never thought I would make it this far.

Here I am standing in the same shoes you stood in for so many years. I just hope I am half as good as you. People still remember you Pops. I've talked to soldiers and the first think they ask me did I know CSM Howard. I tell them, he's my grandfather.

I know I have some heavy shoes to fill, Pops." "Son, you not filling my shoes. What you are doing is walking in your own footprint. You as a CSM has a responsibility and it's not to yourself it's to all your soldiers.

Soldiers look up to their CSM. You represent the command but most of all you represent the soldier that's under your command. Never let anyone tell you anything different no matter what their rank is. Officers will definitely try to remind you that you represent the command.

But, let them know with all due respect, "Sir, I represent all soldier of this command" don't ever forget that. You do not want to become the command's CSM. If that happens your soldiers will know that, and they will lose that belief that you are there for them.

A lot of CSM let that happened once they became CSM and they lose that edge they had with their troops. Soldiers want to believe that they can always depend on their CSM, because you came up through the ranks same as they came through to get where you are. Be stern, be honest and never let your soldiers down. That's all I've got to say. Just keep doing what you been doing. It got you this far.

You've come a long way. You're a young CSM at the age of thirty-four." "Pops, I'm only thirty-three." Well, you still young for a CSM." I walked over and said, "So what's my two most favorite CSMs talking about?" "Oh, nothing much my darling wife, just passing on some wisdom to a very young CSM."

"Ok, I just want to remind you that you did say no shop talk." Looking at my grandson and said, "Just keep in mind you were taught by the best, but then I'm somewhat bias when it comes to your pops."

"So, my dear what are you up to?" "I'm going to take the crew for a walk before it gets too late. You want to come." "No, I'm going to just hang out and check on the other house see how they doing there. So, CSM, who you put with all the kids?" "Charmaine and Jim, they volunteered. I think they wanted to keep an eye on the little ones." "That's a good idea. Jim's real good with them."

I started to walk down the beach with my crew. Chaplain Anderson caught me as I started down the steps. He asked, "Mind some company?" "No, Chaplain not at all." "Please, call me Paul. So tell me, how things been going with the Howard clan as I may say?"

"Things are going real fine. No more than the average family would have." "Now, Val you mind." "Please." "Now Val, your family is not an ordinary family. Your family has really kept me in the ministry business. You are unique but you are a loving group of people who care very much for each other.

But, Val I have a feeling there is some unfinished business that is effecting you and your family. I don't want to sound like some fortune teller, but my spirit lays heavy on a situation with my friend. Is everything alright with Dan?"

"Paul, I don't want to say but maybe you should talk with him if this is something that nags at your spirit. I too am a little concern about him. I know he called you and I don't want to speak of it until he talks with you.

All I'm going to say, it has a lot to do with forgiveness." "Aah, I had a feeling it did. Is it Janelle or is it him or maybe it's both." "Paul,

I'm not going to say any more. Daniel has this thing about me being the Mother hen who's always poking my head around the hen house.

I do tend to get involved in a lot of things when it comes to our family. So I promise myself I was going to stay completely out of this and let him handle it."

"Ok, well is that why he ask me to come up?" "I'm not going to say. I'm going to say this though. Your friend Daniel has this thing about fixing everyone's problem but tend to ignore his own. I'll leave it at that." "I got you." Paul continued with his walk as I turned and walked back to the house.

As I started up the steps Daniel stopped me and ask, "Where you run off to?" As he caught my hand as we walked down the beach. "I took the crew for their evening walk, and Paul asked me could he walk with me."

"So, what did y'all talk about?" "We didn't talk about anything really. He mentioned to me his spirit was very heavy and concerned about his friend."

"Did you mention why I asked him to come up?" "No, I felt that was something you needed to bring up to him." "You sure you didn't tell or mention anything to him." "I'm sure honey, I told myself I was going to stay out of this but, remember what I told you also. You need to forgive her before you can forgive yourself.

Your friend is a very spirit filled person. He is led by the spirit. He knew something was wrong with you and he is not here because you called. He is here because the Holy Spirit led him here. I did not tell him anything. He already knew what it was and what it is.

You best let him know before this whole thing destroys you. You my husband is treading in dangerous water. You need to walk up to your friend Chaplain Anderson and tell him you need to talk with him. He is a man of God he will not steer you wrong. Right now Daniel you are ticking me off. You can help everyone else, but when it comes to you.

You tend to ignore it, unless you are force to do something about it. Just like your situation with DJ's death and with Jim. I'm not going to sit by and let you destroy yourself because you don't want to do something about it." "Val, I am doing something about it." "What than Daniel?" "I'm going to talk to Paul." "When Daniel? When everybody has left and gone their separate ways.

Daniel listen to me, I know you cannot move on without forgiveness. I know that. Forgiveness is not for that individual you are forgiving. Forgiveness is for you. It cleanse your heart, your mind and your soul. I had to do it to get on with my life. Listen to me my darling. When I was stationed down in Seal Beach, CA, I had this attachment that I knew I needed to let go of. Remember the husband I told you about that treated me so badly.

He physically and mentally abused me for almost ten years. I was scared of him. I was in California and he was in Virginia. One day in my apartment I sat there after coming from church.

I told me, self I had to release myself from the thing that held me to this man. So I took a chair and sat it, in my living room. And I sat in that chair and look at that sofa as if he was sitting on that sofa. I told that sofa.

I forgive you. I forgive you for all the things you did to me. I forgive you for the beatings, the black eyes, the swollen lips and the broken arms. I forgive you for dragging me down the steps and causing me to miscarriage.

I forgive you for cutting up my clothes and the way you treated me in front of your family and mine. I forgive you for you taking my hard earn money and spending on yourself and most of all I forgive you for not loving me when I loved you more than myself. Most of all I forgive you so I can forgive myself for being so weak and not strong enough to be strong for myself.

Daniel all though that period I said I forgive the tears rolled down my face. I had to finally ask God to forgive him from being a weak man and not strong enough to be a man. I remember falling to my knees and crying until there was no more tears left to cry. I then got up wiped my eyes and took my dog, Ebony for a long walk along the beach.

As I took that walk I felt an overwhelming feeling of freedom as I looked out at the ocean as the sun began to settle along the ocean.

This Daniel is when I found myself. That strong willed girl who grew up in the projects and wanted to travel and see the world. Forgiveness is for you the one who is forgiving.

Daniel forgiveness makes you a forgiving person. When you talk to Paul he's going to tell you a lot of what I just said. I wanted to tell you all this the other day when we were talking. Unforgiveness creates hate in your heart. I just believe that if you forgive Janelle you will know, but not understand why she could never forgive. I just believe she couldn't forgive because she couldn't forgive herself for why her mother left."

"Ok Val, I'm going to look for Paul now. Since you told me all what you did. I think I understand why you are such a forgiving person." We walk back to the house and ran across Paul on our way back. Daniel said, "Hold up Paul, I need to talk with you." He walked me to the steps, kissed my head and said I won't be too long.

Daniel was gone a little over an hour. When he got back I asked. "How things go" "You were right. He knew I was spiritually in pain. He said he was familiar with what was going on in my mind and heart. Danielle came by to see him a couple of months ago. She was having a hard time dealing with what her mom had done to them and how come she hated her so much and didn't want to forgive her.

She wasn't sure if she should or why she should. She came to visit him right after DJ got married. She felt like she should tell everyone about the kind of person her mother was and how much she hated her. So her husband Paul told her she should go talk to Chaplain Anderson. That's why she went to see him."

"Well, did she do that? Did she forgive Janelle, her mother? Did she forgive her for everything she did to her and her brother?" "Last I talked to Danielle she was not in the forgiving frame of mind. May be Paul convinced her it's something she needs to do in order to have peace of mind. That's what Chaplain Anderson told me.

Well, to make a long story short Chaplain Anderson told me the exact same thing you said. Forgiveness is not for the one you are forgiving it's for you the one who is forgiving. He told me before you forgive a person you need to have a list of what you are forgiving that person for. Call that person name out and tell them you forgive them for whatever that's on that list. You must say this from you heart and you must really forgive them. He said forgiveness is given from the heart.

Your forgiveness is to release you, as the one who is forgiving from that which you are holding in you. If you do not forgive you will become very toxic with that hate because unforgiveness is a form of hate.

Unforgiveness like hate is like a cancer that eats you up from the inside." "So, my question, are you going to forgive Janelle or what? Do you know why you need to forgive her? I don't want to be pushy. But this whole Janelle thing has been tormenting you for almost three years."

"Yes honey, I'm going to do it. It's been eating at me for so long. I'm beginning to let it eat at my train of thought. I'm just not being myself." "Well, ok I'm not going to ask you anymore. I would be able to tell if you have."

CHAPTER

Five

The Fourth of July celebration did not go without any surprises. Tom called and said he was sorry he was not going to make it up for the holiday. He was going up to Seattle because there was an emergency. His oldest son called and said his mother had tried to kill herself.

Daniel still no real love for the lady said, "What she trying to do get her husband back?" Eloise said, "She wrote a letter and said she can't live without her husband Tom. So Tom flew up to Seattle to be with her." Chief looked at Daniel and said, "Tell him to keep in touch."

The three day event was very eventfully. The family watched the firework display on the front deck in lawn chairs. Jim had brought some fireworks and sparklets up from Texas for the kids to do some on the beach. The kids were so excited. As I sat out and watch our little family enjoy their selves. I hadn't notice that Daniel was not out there. I ask Chief where he went to he said he didn't know. I later saw him walking back down the beach. I ask him, "Where did you go?" "I just went for a walk." "You alright?" "Yeah, I just felt like taking a walk. Val, I'm fine really I am."

Since the fourth was Sport's provisional birthday. We decided to have cake and ice cream for him. We all sang happy birthday and let him open up his presents. Already in preschool, he was excited at all the presents he got. Jim let them play until they fell out from exhaustion. He had become a really committed father and grandfather for that matter. He spent a lot of time with the kids. They loved being with him.

I started to go in for the night and let the young people have their fun. I told them not to celebrate too much. Daniel walked up behind me and said, "I love you. Come walk with me," as he caught my hand and we walked down the beach. "Val, I love you so very much. I don't know what my life would be without you.

You have made me one of the happiest people in this world. I'm sorry I was short with you earlier. I didn't mean it the way it came out." "I understand we have our moments" "I look out at our family and extended family and it makes me very happy. We have come a long way my darling. We have overcome some things in our life that would have torn others a part. But we are still a family. Most of that has to do with you. You don't know how much you means to me and this family. We all love you so very much. I really hope you understand that.

Val, I just want you to know I understand and realized what you were telling me about forgiveness. How much I needed to do that. I did just as you said and Chaplain Anderson and it has made a difference in how I feel about Janelle. I had to try to find a way to forgive myself. Well, that's where I was a little while ago. I had to forgive myself for the selfish things I did like abandoning my children and leaving them with a women I knew had some mental issues.

I had to forgive myself for not removing my children from a toxic environment which I knew was toxic. I finally had to forgive myself for not loving myself enough to be strong enough to make those changes I knew needed to be made. I actually was a weak person during that period in my life when I thought I was strong. So, in saying all that, I and instead of being mad at Janelle and myself I had to forgive both of us. Believe me Val, that was what I really needed to face my own errors in that marriage and forgive myself.

But I did not forgive myself for falling in love with you or ever meeting you. Paul told me the other day. You might have made a mistake with Janelle but, Val was never a mistake in your life. When one door closes another opens. Val was your open door. Val, you open the door to a whole new life for me. A life, I may not have never had if you had not come back into my life that day in Arlington.

Here it is almost ten years later and I still love you as it was the first day I saw you in Presidio. No one could ever love you as much as I love you. I never wanted anything in my life as much as I want you in my life. So, my darling wife I ask for your forgiveness for not appreciating you for sharing my life with me." He then kissed me so hard and tender.

I then said, "I forgive you but there was never a reason for forgiveness. I have a lot of faith in you and I have always believed in you. I've always believed that faith tells you to believe in something when common sense tells you not too. I've always had more faith in you than common sense. If that was so I would have never been at Arlington that day.

On the day which brought you to me and me to you. Some would've called it KAMA but I called it God. Now here we are still in love with each other more than ever. I love you my husband more than life itself. I've never felt this way about anyone I've been involved with."

We walked back towards the summer house. We ran into DJ and Trinity. "Where you two love birds been," asked DJ. "We just went for a walk and watch the surfs come in. We usually do this every night before we turn in." Daniel offered. "How you doing Trinity?" "Oh, I doing just fine. Danielle suggested I take a walk at least once a day. That's if I can get up. If I'd known marrying into a family which spits out twins I might had thought twice about marrying this guy over here." "How I know. I wasn't a twin." "But your dad was and I see it runs in the family" "Well, it's too late now." "When the twins due?" Daniel asked. "Not soon enough," DJ offered. "Well, you can come and stay with us awhile.

You'll be near the clinic where Danielle is and we're used to having pregnant women around the mansion. Aren't we honey?" I offered "Sure we'll love to have you there. When your leave over CSM." "I took two week off to do some things around the house. It'll be great if Trinity is in El Paso. That way I won't be worried about her being alone. When y'all going back to El Paso?" "We were planning on staying here for the rest of the week and fly home Friday." "I can stick around for that long. That way my beautiful wife (as he winked) can take her daily walks. I'll be here to encourage her."

"You mean push me to walk." "That's ok honey, you can be mean to me I still love you." "So I guess it's settled. Y'all going to stick around for a few days. That way you and your pops can hang out and do something you haven't done in years since you joined the Army. Trinity and I can relax for the next few days." "That sounds great." "Well, now that we got that settled. I guess we'll turn in. Go night y'all." "Good night Pops, Nana," as he kissed me.

Eloise called to let Daniel know Tom was going to be in Seattle a while. He didn't know when he'll be back because of her condition. Daniel said he'll call him tomorrow.

The next day Daniel called Tom and found Diane had taken a turn for the worse. He decided to take a leave of absence and stay in the area with his son who is in the Army. He had pretty much blamed his self for all that his wife was going through. He told him Diane was never a very strong minded person. She spent most of their life together trying to impress her father because she married an African American.

He spent his time trying to help her impress him. He said he never liked him but he loved his wife. She got involved in a lot of things that she shouldn't had, but she thought she was doing a good thing. She got caught up in matters that she shouldn't. Like your marriage to Janelle. Janelle was the only real friend she had. She knew Janelle was using her to get back at you but she didn't care. She was her so called friend.

When Janelle told her she had cancer she became even closer. Not because she was her friend or anything else, but because Diane really didn't have any friend since she had married me. She would do anything she could to keep that friendship. Janelle told her when I die you can have my house since you are my best friend. I don't think anything came of it.

Until recently, when she came back here she had burned so many bridges with her father and mother as they said because of me. She was not allowed there. She told him about the house which you had demoed and that's when they got the lawyers involved. She got so furious with me she said if you and your company meant that much than she was going to file for divorce and move back to Seattle.

When she moved back she had nowhere to go since she had almost caused my oldest son and his wife to breakup. If you can remember by daughter-in-law is also African American. She told him why you married her you're white. So a lot went on about that so she was not welcome. That's Thomas my oldest son who called and told me mother is in the hospital she tried to kill herself.

So, I get here and I am told she been living in a hotel because she couldn't find a place to live. This I didn't know. I called her father. He didn't want to talk to me because he said I dragged her down there with all those you know what type of people and let them destroy his daughter. We had a few words and I let him know his racial prejudices is what destroyed his daughter.

She did not know where she belonged. But when she was with me in Texas she had a very good life she just didn't know how to handle it. That was mainly because you always made her feel she had disgrace your family by marrying a black man. She had a very good life here but you did not let her enjoy it. I told them you are the reason your daughter is in the hospital hanging on for her life.

They alienated her to the point she was ready to give up. She didn't have to tell me. I lived with her for over thirty years and she was never accepted by her father or his family because she married a black man. A man who loved her very much. Even with us going through this divorce Dan, I still love my wife. I just have to be here for her when she wakes up and I can take her home where I have kept her safe from her own kind.

That's why I took the job at HIE, I thought it would be what we needed to get away from her people especially her father and his prejudices. She told me that if she divorced me her father would love her again. She actually believed that. I told her your father does love you but you are considered an embarrassment to who he is and who he represents.

A divorce cannot fix who and what your father is. I've served and been around his type my whole military career. He is a racist and he doesn't like anyone who isn't the color of his skin. He just tolerates us because he is a colonel and he wears the US Army uniform. His biggest problem and your biggest mistake is that you tarnish him and who he is by marrying a black man.

She called me a few weeks ago and told me I was right. Her father told her if she hadn't married that "colored boy" you would not be in the predicament you're in now. She said he runs a billion dollar corporation. He told her he didn't care. They all are crooks as far as he's concern." "Man, he called you colored, I haven't heard that since I was in high school. Go on man I'm listening." "The whole thing he was upset because I was able to pull away from that noose he had on me.

All the time I was at his office I was his "gofer" his little minion for his company. Here I was retired from the Army as a Command Sergeant Major and he treated me like someone who just came out of college. The best thing ever happened to me was you offering me that job.

I would have still been there kissing his butt, and making less than the youngest person in the company. Well, thanks man for making me a part of your corporation. I'll try to get back as soon as I can." "Well, Eloise, Chief, and Jim I'm sure can hold down the fort until you get back. I hope and pray man everything works out for the both of you.

Give her our love and tell her we'll keep her in our prayer." "Wow, man you getting a little spiritual on me?" "Well, man I guess I am. After that ordeal with Janelle and the forgiveness thing I went through. I guess I have changed or it changed my way of thinking and feeling. Keep us in touch on what's going on." He hung up.

Danielle and Paul stopped by before they flew back to El Paso to check on Trinity. Danielle and Daniel had a talk about how she felt about her mother and she was a little apprehensive about the advice

Chaplain Anderson gave her because she had gotten to the point that she really hated her mother.

She said he asked her how she felt about her father being that he was never there. He asked her when he was there why didn't she tell him what was happening. May be if he had known he would have taken you two with him.

He asked her did you ever ask your father could you go with him. She said when daddy was home they would always argue about things she didn't take care of and he would say why you don't go back where your whores are.

He was always trying to explain to her if she was so concern about who he was with then come live with me on the post. She would say, she not going anywhere she doesn't know anybody.

He asked her many times to go and she said she had friend there so she wanted to stay here. Mother didn't have any friends only the ones that came around and drank and got high with her. She had men came by the house and she would say they were daddy's friends.

But when daddy came home none of them came by. That's when I knew she was lying. We wanted to tell you daddy but we were scared what she might do to us. Every time you left she was nice for a day or two. Then she be her old self again. Mad because you wouldn't have sex with her and kept saying you had some women you had living with you and start throwing things. I understand daddy, mother was mean to you. It was almost as if she was trying to make you leave when you came.

Only time we got a hot meal was when you came home and you cooked it. All the other times it was frozen food. DJ would put something in the microwave oven and we would eat in our room. She never took us out to eat. Sometimes she would buy us McDonald's or Popeye's because they were close by. She told us if your father come and try to take you. I'll tell the police he's a child molester.

Daddy she was the child molester." "Well, did you forgive your mother?" "I did. I had to forgive her for all that she did to me and DJ. I think DJ forgave her a long time ago. I remember DJ called me one time when I was in college and told me.

Babe sister you have to forgive mama for all the things she did to us and try to go on with your life. I told him I hated her and I'll never forgive her. I hope she die before I do that. That's why he was able to go on with his life. Daddy DJ was so much like you. I remember when we ran away that time. He said that's ok I'm going to join the Army and find daddy.

When he got older and went in the Army he was just like you. He even act and walked like you. He even had this thing about winking his eye. He reminded me so much of you. When I was in Grad school he called me every weekend to see if I was ok. He sent me money even though I didn't need it.

Yeah pops, I think he forgave her a long time ago. That's why he was able to get married and get on with his life. He had forgiven her."

"That's one thing I must say about your twin he was definitely a good man. He knew he had to forgive her to get on with his life. Now that we have forgiven her and our self, we can get on with our life. The kids all grown up and moving on with their life. We have a lot to be thankful for."

"Now, I've got to go and check on my patient before I leave. Understand she's going to be staying at the mansion. She's very close. There might be another set of twins born there before you know it." "Well, we're flying back to El Paso on Friday.

DJ is flying back with us also. He wants to make sure she's settled in before he goes back to Fort Hood. They never told us what they were." "Oh, maybe I should leave that up to DJ."

DJ walked in and said, "Leave what up to DJ?" "What you having son?" "Oh, I didn't tell you pops. Twin boys" "Two more Sergeant Majors in the family. Hey Val, they're having twin boys." "I knew that. I was waiting for him to tell you." "You knew!!" "Yeah, I knew that would make you happy."

"Well, son looks like you broke the cycle with twin boys." "I guess I did pops. I'm going up and check on her. She always wants me with her when Dr. Danielle comes by." "Dr. Danielle." I said, "Honey, everybody calls her that even her patients. She said it make her feel closer to her patients. She a very good Pediatrician."

LOVE, LIFE'S ENDLESS DESTINY

Danielle came back down and said, "Well, I might have to stick around her a little longer. Look like those little guys ready to check the world out. She's having contractions. I knew that walk would do her some good." "Where's DJ?" "He upstairs with her." "I'm so proud of him.

That boy just like you daddy. He has your same demeanor. He's going to be right there with her until those babies get here." "Well, we've been through this before." "Paul honey, you can go tell JT, we won't be going anywhere today." "Well, the company's on vacation this week anyway. So, there's really no used in rushing back unless they got something to do. I'll give Chief a call and see what his schedule looks like."

The phone rang Chief said, "I was just about to give you a call." "What's up" "Tom called. Diane past away about a couple of hours ago. He wants to bring her body down to El Paso and bury her." "So what's the problem? Go up there and get her." "It's not that simple. Diane's family wants to cremate her." "Why?" "He doesn't know. He thinks it's something about he's the cause her committing suicide.

So they don't want him to come to the memorial service. Also they were in the process of getting a divorce." "But she had never filed for one." "So her family is getting a lawyer to keep Tom from bring her body back to El Paso. I think he's going to need some help on this. He's desperate. His sons want her buried down there also. But they haven't talked to the family in years. So, they are not on good turns with their so called grandparents."

"So, Chief what's your plan?" "How you figure I have a plan." "Because you didn't tell me that if you haven't figured out a way to fix this." "Well, I've already made some calls. I got a judge to release her body to her husband and we're on our way up there to pick him up and Diane's remains and I need you to go with me.

Just in case those redneck see fit to cause a little trouble. I have a buddy who's a Washington State trooper is going to escort her remains to SEATAC. All we have to do is pick up Tom and meet them at the airport." "Why can't he meet us at the airport?" "He has to sign for the release of her remains."

When are wheels up?" "In a couple of hours, I'm taking JT as back up in case we have some problem there." "Man, I can't believe we're going through all this knowing what Diane put this company through." "Dan this isn't about Diane or her family. It's about Tom and Tom is family. He loved Diane and she loved him. It was her family that created their problems.

I think two of his sons and their family is coming back also. JT's going to transport the family and we're going to transport Tom and Diane's remains." "Well, look like you got a plan. Give me a moment to tell Val what's going on and I'll grab my to-go-bag."

The flight was a four hour flight into SEATAC. The holdup was when Tom tried to sign for Diane's remains. They had to wait for the court release to arrive at the hospital morgue. Diane's father was still very persistent about not letting Tom take her body back to El Paso.

Once the sheriff deputy arrived, they were very cooperative after the deputy showed them the court order releasing the remains to her immediate husband. The trip to El Paso was a very solemn ride. Once JT deplaned the family he refueled headed the back to Virginia.

Daniel arrived just in time to witness the birth of his great grandsons. DJ and AJ, Daniel Jarrell Howard IV and Antonio Jamal II. They were almost identical. Except DJ had a birthmark on his right arm and AJ didn't have any noticeable one yet. I looked at my baby DJ and said, "Now you are a father and I'm so proud of you. You still my baby."

"Yeah Nana, we now have a fourth generation of DJ Howard and a second of AJ Howard." Daniel came in and asked, "Where those new great grandsons of mine." DJ said, "Pops meet DJ and AJ Howard the next generation of the Howard's clan."

I asked him, "How things go?" "They went very well, considering the source. We got everyone back in El Paso and the families. I think the funeral is going to be on Saturday or Sunday. We should be back home by then." "I said that's good. I glad you got Diane's remains back home to El Paso. She was unhappy but she was at home whether she knew it or not."

"Val, the only reason she was unhappy because her father couldn't forgive her for marrying a black man. A man she loved and the man that loved her and not because of the color of his skin.

You would think by now people would have learned that it's not about the color of their skin but the contents of who they are as a person. Tom is a good man and he gave up a long time ago on Diane's family when they called his first son the "N-word".

I guess he wasn't white enough for them. I'm so glad children today are growing up in a different frame of minds. They only know this by the spelling or pronunciation of their names."

"When Trinity and Krystyna was going to school. They never had a problem about race unless they see it on TV. They never questioned it. They have friends of various nationalities and they were welcome to their houses as well as our home.

I truly believe the thing about race and color of the skin is going to be a thing of the past if we continue to do what we are doing. Raise our children without a perspective of color or national origin."

"Val, its people like Diane's father who can't let go of the past. They believe in a supreme race and they are that supreme race. They believe their God made them the supreme race over all mankind.

They came to this country to be dominant over all mankind." "So, what do you believe?" "I'm not sure but I want to believe we are here to show the world that we as a country; can be a strong country that's governed by the citizens of this country through those we elected by those citizens.

Not by those who can buy this country's leadership." "Well, honey you are a billionaire, do you feel you have a right to buy someone into the leadership of this country." "As a billionaire, hell no. America doesn't belong to us billionaires, it belongs to the American tax paying citizens.

This country was never meant to be owned by anyone group of people." "But honey, you fall into that group of people." "Yes I do, but I once and is still one of those tax paying citizen.

Just because I am a self-made billionaire does mean I have a right to control the county I live in. Val, if I lost everything I have as far as money, I would still be a very happy content person. You know why because I know how to make it again. I became a billionaire through hard work and the skills I was taught in the military.

I took those skills and used it for my best benefits. That's where I am today. I never took a dime from the American government without earning it. I will never take a single penny of it to buy the government. America is the land of opportunity and it gave me my opportunity and if anything I owe it."

"Well, you hungry? Soup left a lot of leftover in the kitchen. Since it's just a few of us here we'll have some potluck tonight." As we walked in the kitchen Soup and Jai was still here. Daniel asked, "What you two still doing here?" "Now y'all know I'm not going anywhere until you two leave, and yes we're having pot luck for lunch. I see we have two more mouths to feed around here." Asia started to bark, "not you girl," said Soup. "JT told me y'all been on a couple excursions. I'm really sorry to hear about Diane. How's Tom doing?" Jai asked "He's handling it considering the reason behind it. How long you two going to stick around here?" Daniel asked.

"I think we're all going to fly out together. I understand the funeral is Friday or Saturday," She said. "There might be a little trouble the day of the funeral. We may need to take a bit of precaution." "Why you think that CSM?" asked Soup.

"Well, Diane's family was not too favorable about Tom laying her to rest her in the company's resting place. He may try something. He wanted to cremate her but Tom wouldn't stand for it. He wasn't too happy the way we went about getting the authority involved in bringing her back to El Paso. So that's where we stand as of now." "So, CSM what the story on this man?"

"Well, from our investigation he is someone they call "The Col". He was a Colonel in the Army but got drummed out because of his association with one of the white supremacy group up in the Fort Lewis, area. He owns his own business and Tom worked for him until I hired him with us. So, make a long story short he doesn't like Tom and you can imagine why. He tormented Diane for years for marrying a black man. He is mad with Diane because she wanted to go back to her husband.

We believe Diane took her own life because she felt she couldn't live without her husband Tom. Her father feels she has disgrace him and what he stand for I imagine. So according to him, she doesn't deserve a burial. She should be cremated. That's what they plan to do. His group is on the watch list up in Washington State.

Chief has notified the authorities in the El Paso area. But keep in mind these groups tend to work together. I just want you to understand they are not after us nor Tom. They only want Diane's remains." Jai asked, "Why don't you just give it to them." "Jai, I know there was no love lost between the most of us and Diane. Diane was Tom's wife. That makes her a part of the HIE family. He and his wife has the right to be buried here at HIE's resting place we have for them.

So, as family of HIE and for Tom we will stand by him to lay his wife to rest. I am not going to exercise my rights as CEO of the company, but I hope I made myself clear." Everyone agreed. "Jai would you notify your people we will be leaving tomorrow morning destination El Paso.

The next morning we loaded up the two new additions to the family and the remnant of us from the Fourth of July celebration and flew back to El Paso. We all settled back into the mansion and prepared for what may be a very interesting memorial service for Diane.

Tom and Chief met with Daniel at the COC to go over what was expected during the upcoming event. Tom was a little concern because of who we now called "The COL" may try to do. Tom asked would it be in all our best interest to entomb her at night. In case The COL might try to take the body. Once the body in placed in the tomb on sacred ground on a government installation it is a federal crime to desecrate the grave or tomb of that site.

They had agreed it was in the best interest of everyone involved or who was to attend the memorial service. She would lay in rest and her immediate and certain invites would attend the entombment.

Being the gentleman Tom was, he invited Diane's family to attend her memorial service.

The memorial service was held at the chapel on Fort Bliss. Chaplain Anderson did the service. Diane's mother, sister and oldest brother attended the memorial service. All able employees of HIE was in attendance. It was a very crowded attendance. Diane body laid in rest at the chapel as we all filed out. Diane's father and about six of his people stood outside the chapel as we all filed out.

He then approached Tom and said, "As a citizen of these United States, I demand that you release my daughter's remains to me." Tom said, "Sir I regret to inform you. My wife, your daughter has already been laid to rest." He then walked away as the military police approach the COL and said, Sir you are under arrest for violation of trespassing on government property. He then read him his rights as he handcuffed him and his six followers.

Later that evening we and Diane's mother, sister and brother along with her three sons and their families attended a candlelight visual entombing her next to where her husband one day will be placed. We all left as Tom stayed to say his last good-byes to his wife of over thirty years.

The next day Daniel and I took the jet back to the summer house. We took long walks along the beach with the crew as much as we could. As the sun set over the other side of the house we set in our favorite chaise reminiscing of our life together and the events of the last few days, a birth of two beautiful great grandsons. The loss of a friend thinking of how much she was torn between two loves.

The love she had for her husband and the love she desired so much from her father. I look at my husband and said, "I'm glad you are such a loving person. You are my strength that keeps me wanting to keep our family together. I thank God every moment I can for bringing you into my life. We are surely blessed my husband" He held my hand, kissed it and said, "That we are my wife."

As we continue to spend our days at the summer house just us two and the crew I can't help but think back how our life together has somewhat meant to happen.

LOVE, LIFE'S ENDLESS DESTINY

I thought how unintentionally I met a wonderful man I had fell in love with, at a critical time in our country's history, who changed my life eternally. Now here I am married to that wonderful man, who fulfills my dream and love me more than life itself. Our love has become a life of an endless destiny. A life that is still on its journey.

A Love that each night I go to sleep beside my husband I know I have finally found what it is like to have that eternal loved one that so many never fines. I found that love in the man I followed half way across the globe and back. In that man, who never stopped loving me when we were apart decades. The man, who never stop waiting for a love he had never given up on. When I had given up on a love I had thought I lost in a war that we thought would never end.

The love of a man whom groomed into a family of his own, those who he never forgot and he cared about that made a mark in his life. A man, who loved his friends as if they were his immediate family. As I look at my husband, I think of the wonders he has done with the love he has for his family, our grandchildren and great grandchildren.

To think it all started in that beautiful penthouse apartment in San Francisco that overlooks the beautiful city by the bay, high above the fog that slowly moves into the city each night like that mysterious lady looking for a one night stand. She was my friend and he was my lover. An eternal love that has no end.

The End

Soon to be Release

Forever My Love

My Forbidden Love – A Soldier's Love Story

Continuing Saga

Love, Our Eternal Promise

Love, Life's Eternal Flame

and

Love, Life's Endless Destiny

Printed in the USA
CPSIA information can be obtained
at www.ICGtesting.com
LVHW021400051023
760085LV00064B/2203